Most Wanted

✳ HOLIDAY HUNKS ✳

AN ARCHWAY PAPERBACK
Published by **POCKET BOOKS**

New York   **London**   **Toronto**   **Sydney**   **Tokyo**   **Singapore**

AN ARCHWAY PAPERBACK *Original*

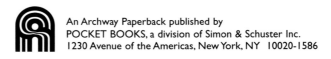

An Archway Paperback published by
POCKET BOOKS, a division of Simon & Schuster Inc.
1230 Avenue of the Americas, New York, NY 10020-1586

ISBN: 0-671-02665-8

First Archway Paperback printing December 1998

10 9 8 7 6 5 4 3 2 1

AN ARCHWAY PAPERBACK and colophon are registered trademarks of Simon & Schuster Inc.

Printed in the U.S.A.

COVER PHOTO CREDITS:
front top left, Tonge/RP/Retna; front top right, Photofest; front bottom left, Gallo/Retna; front bottom right, Kwaku Alston/Outline; back top left, Photofest; back top right, Beckman/Retna; back bottom, Alpha/Globe Photos

Backstreet Boys

LAST PROJECT: Their self-titled debut CD

CURRENTLY WORKING ON: Touring around the United States and Canada

ALEXANDER JAMES McLEAN

NICKNAME: A.J.

BORN: January 9, 1978 in West Palm Beach, Florida

SIGN: Capricorn

FAMILY: Parents Denise and Robert

EYES: Brown

HAIR: Dark brown

FAVORITE:
- MUSIC: Barrie McKnight
- FOOD: Fast-food burgers
- COLOR: Purple

ON STARDOM: "We want people to know our first priority is good music."

BRIAN THOMAS LITTRELL

NICKNAME: B-Rok

BORN: February 20, 1975 in Lexington, Kentucky

SIGN: Pisces

FAMILY: Parents Jackie and Harold Littrell, brother Harold Jr.

EYES: Blue

HAIR: Blond

FAVORITE:
- MUSIC: Boyz II Men
- FOOD: Macaroni and cheese
- COLOR: Forest green

ON STARDOM: "Since we've started, we've been really lucky with some of the people who support us—we've got some brillant fans."

HOWARD DWAINE DOROUGH

NICKNAME: Howie D.

BORN: August 22, 1973 in Orlando, Florida

SIGN: Leo

FAMILY: Parents Paula and Hoke, brother John, and sisters Pollyanna, Caroline, and Angie

EYES: Blue

HAIR: Dark brown

FAVORITE:
- MUSIC: Jon Secada, Bobby Brown
- FOOD: Asian
- COLOR: Purple

ON STARDOM: "Hopefully, we can move people with our music and bring some happiness into other people's lives"

KEVIN SCOTT RICHARDSON

NICKNAME: Kevin

BORN: October 3, 1972 in Lexington, Kentucky

SIGN: Libra

FAMILY: His mom Ann and his late father Jerald, brothers Jerald Jr. and Tim

EYES: Brown

HAIR: Brown

FAVORITE:
- MUSIC: R. Kelly, Babyface, Prince
- FOOD: Asian
- COLOR: Royal blue

ON STARDOM: "We're touching people's lives and making people forget about their problems for a moment. That's what music's all about, I think."

NICKOLAS GENE CARTER

NICKNAME: Nick

BORN: January 28, 1980 in Jamestown, New York

SIGN: Aquarius

FAMILY: Parents Jane and Bob; sisters Bobbi Jean, Lesley, and Angel; brother Aaron

EYES: Blue

HAIR: Blond

FAVORITE:
- MUSIC: Nirvana, Oasis, Jodeci
- FOOD: Pizza
- COLOR: Green

ON STARDOM: "[The fame] hasn't really taken effect on me. I haven't felt it yet. It takes a while...."

The Guys from
Buffy the Vampire Slayer™

NICHOLAS BRENDON

Nickname: Nicky

Born: April 12, 1971 in Los Angeles, California

Sign: Aries

Family: Twin brother named Kelly

Eyes: Hazel

Hair: Brown

Height: 5' 11"

Who He Plays on *Buffy*: Xander LaVelle Harris

DAVID BOREANAZ

Born: May 16, 1971 in Buffalo, New York

Sign: Taurus

Family: Father Dave Roberts is a TV weatherman in Philadelphia

Eyes: Brown

Hair: Brown

Height: 6' 1"

Currently Working On: *Angel* spin-off series

On Stardom: "It's amazing how this show has taken off. I'm blessed with doing *Buffy*. I just have to count those blessings and work hard."

Who He Plays on *Buffy*: Angel (a.k.a. Angelus)

SETH GREEN

Born: September 8, 1974 in Philadelphia, Pennsylvania

Sign: Virgo

Eyes: Blue-green

Hair: Auburn

Major Credits: *Radio Days, Austin Powers, Can't Hardly Wait, Enemy of the State*

Currently Working On: *Idle Hands*

Who He Plays on *Buffy*: Oz

Aaron Carter

BORN: December 7, 1987

SIGN: Sagittarius

FAMILY: Parents Jane and Bob; sisters Bobbi Jean, Lesley, and his twin, Angel; brother Nick of the Backstreet Boys

EYES: Brown

HAIR: Blond

HEIGHT: 4'6"

MAJOR CREDITS: Self-titled debut album

CURRENTLY WORKING ON: Touring with the Backstreet Boys

FAVORITE:

MUSIC: Babyface

FOOD: Pizza with anchovies

ON STARDOM: "Being able to meet my fans, going around the world and visiting countries...it's a good feeling because no other ten-year-old boy gets to perform on stage and do stuff like that."

Matthew Paige Damon

NICKNAME: Matt

BORN: October 8, 1970 in Cambridge, Massachusetts

SIGN: Libra

FAMILY: Parents Nancy Carlsson-Paige and Kent Damon, brother Kyle

EYES: Blue

HAIR: Light brown

HEIGHT: 5'10"

MAJOR CREDITS: *Good Will Hunting, Saving Private Ryan, Rounders*

CURRENTLY WORKING ON: *Dogma, The Talented Mr. Ripley*

FAVORITE MOVIE: *Tender Mercies*

ON STARDOM: "My family doesn't let me get away with anything. They bring me back down to earth and make me realize that my fame doesn't absolve me of being a good human being."

Leonardo Wilhelm DiCaprio

✳ Actor ✳

NICKNAME: Leo

BORN: November 11, 1974 in Los Angeles, California

SIGN: Scorpio

FAMILY: Parents George and Irmelin DiCaprio, stepbrother Adam Starr

EYES: Blue-green

HAIR: Blond

HEIGHT: 6'

MAJOR CREDITS: *Titanic, What's Eating Gilbert Grape, William Shakespeare's Romeo + Juliet, Celebrity*

FAVORITE:

    MUSIC: Beatles, Pink Floyd, Led Zeppelin

    MOVIE: *The Godfather Trilogy*

    FOOD: Pasta

    COLOR: Green

ON STARDOM: "I don't care about being a huge star. I care about being an actor."

Jakob Dylan

 **Musician**

BORN: 1969 in New York City

FAMILY: Father Bob Dylan is a music legend

EYES: Blue

HAIR: Brown

MAJOR CREDITS: The lead singer of The Wallflowers; *Bringing Down the Horse* (Interscope Records)

ON STARDOM: "Absolutely, I think the name [Dylan] worked against me. And I actually found some kind of power in that. I still do. I do not mope, and I do not complain. I've driven my own path here, and I'm on it, and it's fine. But if people think it must be easy…"

Hanson

Last Projects: *Three Car Garage, Middle of Nowhere*

Currently Working On: Touring and recording their next album

CLARKE ISAAC HANSON

Nickname: Ike

Born: November 17, 1980

Sign: Scorpio

Eyes: Brown

Hair: Dark blond

Favorite color: Green

On Stardom: "We love making music, and we love what we're doing. We love where we are, and we want to keep doing it for the rest of our lives."

JORDAN TAYLOR HANSON

Nickname: Tay

Born: March 14, 1983

Sign: Pisces

Eyes: Blue

Hair: Blond

Favorite color: Red

On Stardom: "Music can't be about fame and money or any of that stuff. You have to really love it."

ZACHARY WALKER HANSON

Nickname: Zac

Born: October 22, 1985

Sign: Libra

Eyes: Brown

Hair: Blond

Favorite color: Blue

On Stardom: "You can't expect success. You can only hope for it."

Matt LeBlanc

BORN: July 25, 1967 in Newton, Massachusetts

SIGN: Leo

PETS: His dog, Lady

EYES: Brown

HAIR: Brown

MAJOR CREDITS: Joey on *Friends, Lost in Space* (the movie)

Jared Leto

BORN: December 26, 1971 in Bossier City, Louisiana

SIGN: Capricorn

EYES: Blue

HAIR: Brown

HEIGHT: 6'

MAJOR CREDITS: Jordan Catalano on *My So-Called Life*, *Prefontaine*

CURRENTLY WORKING ON: *The Thin Red Line*, *Basil*, *Urban Legend*

FAVORITE:

   MUSIC: Nirvana, Marilyn Manson

   FOOD: Popcorn

ON STARDOM: "I got lucky really soon, so I'm still trying to learn what I'm doing. I'm learning in front of the camera."

His Royal Highness Prince William Arthur Philip Louis

NICKNAMES: Prince William, Wills

BORN: June 21, 1982 in London, England

SIGN: Gemini

FAMILY: Parents His Royal Highness Prince Charles of Wales and the late Princess Diana, brother His Royal Highness Prince Henry Charles Albert David, usually called Harry

EYES: Blue

HAIR: Blond

HEIGHT: 6' 1"

WHAT THE FUTURE HOLDS: William will most likely become His Royal Highness The Prince of Wales when his father becomes king.

FAVORITE:

    BOOKS: Action-adventure fiction and nonfiction

    MUSIC: Pop music, especially techno

    MOVIES: Action films

    FOOD: Fast-food

Freddie Prinze, Jr.

BORN: March 8, 1976

SIGN: Pisces

FAMILY: Father the late Freddie Prinze, Sr. was the star of TV's *Chico and the Man*

EYES: Brown

HAIR: Brown

MAJOR CREDITS: *I Know What You Did Last Summer, I Still Know What You Did Last Summer, To Gillian on Her 37th Birthday, The House of Yes*

CURRENTLY WORKING ON: *Wing Commander, She's All That, Sparkler*

Willard Smith, Jr.

✳ Actor/Musician ✳

Nicknames: Will Smith, The Fresh Prince

Born: September 25, 1968 in Philadelphia, Pennsylvania

Sign: Libra

Family: Parents Caroline and Willard Smith, Sr., sisters Pam and Ellen, brother Harry

Eyes: Brown

Hair: Brown

Height: 6'3"

Major Credits: *Enemy of the State, The Fresh Prince of Bel Air, Independence Day, Bad Boys, Men in Black, Big Willie Style* (CD)

Currently working on: *The Wild Wild West, The Mark*

Favorite:

Book: *Before the Mayflower: A History of Black America,* by Lerone Bennett

Music: Mariah Carey, Bobby Brown

Movies: Action movies and anything directed by Spike Lee or John Singleton

Food: Burgers and fries

On Stardom: "Music is the most difficult creative form. Music is like a baby, you gotta nurture it, every second of your life has to be dedicated to the music. It's really a huge undertaking."

James William Van Der Beek

* Actor *

Nickname: Baby James

Born: March 8, 1977 in Cheshire, Connecticut

Sign: Pisces

Eyes: Hazel

Hair: Blond

Height: 6'

Major credits: Dawson Leary on *Dawson's Creek*

Currently working on: *Harvest, Varsity Blues*

Favorite:

> **Book:** *Portrait of the Artist as a Young Man by James Joyce*
>
> **Color:** Blue

Scott Wolf

NICKNAME: Scooter

BORN: June 4, 1968 in Boston, Massachusetts

SIGN: Gemini

FAMILY: Parents Steven Wolf and Susan Enowitch, brothers Michael and Gary, sister Jessica

EYES: Blue

HAIR: Brown

HEIGHT: 5' 8"

MAJOR CREDITS: Bailey Salinger on *Party of Five, White Squall*

CURRENTLY WORKING ON: *Go, Cross Country*

FAVORITE:

    BOOKS: *Misery, 100 Years of Solitude, Siddhartha*

    MUSIC: Buffalo Tom, Smashing Pumpkins, Stone Temple Pilots, Lisa Loeb

    MOVIE: *Rainman*

    FOODS: Sushi, pizza

    COLOR: Green

Tiger Woods

FIRST NAME: Eldrick

BORN: December 20, 1975 in Cypress, California

SIGN: Sagittarius

FAMILY: Parents Earl and Kultida Woods

EYES: Brown

HAIR: Black

HEIGHT: 6' 1"

MAJOR ACCOMPLISHMENTS: In 1997 he became the youngest Masters Tournament champion in history and the first major championship winner of African or Asian heritage.

ON STARDOM: "I know my goal is to obviously be the best player in the world. I know that's a very lofty goal, but if I try to accomplish that goal and I do, great. If I don't, I tried. I expect nothing but the best for myself."